Granny and Me

by Robin Ballard

GREENWILLOW BOOKS

NEW YORK

Pen and ink and watercolors were used for the full-color art.
The text type is Korinna.

Printed in Singapore by Tien Wah Press

First Edition   10 9 8 7 6 5 4 3 2 1

Library of Congress Cataloging-in-Publication Data

Ballard, Robin.
  Granny and Me / by Robin Ballard.
     p.   cm.
  Summary: Annie describes some of the activities
that she and her grandmother do together,
including looking at family photographs.
  ISBN 0-688-10548-3.
  ISBN 0-688-10549-1 (lib. bdg.)
  [1. Grandmothers—Fiction.]   I. Title.
PZ7.B2125Gr   1992
[E]—dc20   90-24170   CIP   AC

FOR MY GRANNY BEE

AND

MY GRANNY WOOLF

This is me, Annie, and this is my grandmother.
I like to visit her place, and I like the things
we do together.

Sometimes we ride around in her car,
not very fast, not far.

We often go to the beach, where
Granny reads me stories.

Sometimes in the evening we bake
star-shaped cookies.

Or maybe I dress up in Granny's beautiful clothes.

But my favorite time with Granny is
when we look at all the family photos.

Granny knows who everybody is.

George 1889

In our family there was a smuggler named
Bobo who sailed up and down the coast,
and a scientist who found a cure
for sick chickens.

There was a Cherokee Indian whose
hair grew down to her heels,
and a circus clown.
He was my great-grandfather.

During a circus show he met my great-grandmother.
Soon they were married. This is their daughter.
She's my granny.

They lived on a farm in the middle of the land.

Granny fell in love with the baker.

She says I bake as well as he.

Later my mother was born.

When Mama grew up, she went to the city.

There she met my father.

Here's a picture of my parents.

I study the pictures to find someone
who looks like me. I look for my eyes.
I look for my nose.

"Who's this, Granny?" I ask, and she says,

"Why, Annie, that's you as a baby."

We put the pictures away for another time.

And Granny gets the camera out.

Later we talk and eat our star-shaped cookies.

Then Granny tucks me in for the night.

I love my grandmother,
and I love the things
we do together.